Stuck in the Mud

Brittany Sloan Fergus
Illustrated by: Cait Chiou

ISBN: 978-1-960146-73-1 (hard cover)
ISBN: 978-1-960146-74-8 (soft cover)

Edited by: Amy Ashby

Warren
publishing

Published by Warren Publishing
Charlotte, NC
www.warrenpublishing.net
Printed in the United States

For Jonathan and Rowan

One morning, from the kitchen window, seven-year-old Jonathan spotted something in the peaceful, muddy marsh he called his backyard. Jonathan was ever the marsh scout, and any changes to the horizon were obvious to his watchful eye. This new sighting made him very curious.

After a few more bites of peanut butter toast, he dug out his yellow binoculars and ran outside to the backyard. Jonathan's golden retriever, Rowan, followed behind, his copper fur shiny in the morning sunlight. They waved to Regina and Michael next door who were floating in their pool while their puppy, Nyo, sunned himself on the patio. Rowan and Jonathan perched themselves between two palmetto trees that lined their backyard.

The crosswinds whistled through the leaves of the trees as Jonathan peered through his binoculars. He could see the rugged shells of the endless oyster beds that dotted the marsh. As he scanned slowly, inch-by-inch through the binoculars, the object that had caught Jonathan's eye came into focus! It was a sailboat!

Every morning and afternoon, Jonathan checked for the sailboat. Each day, it remained in the same spot. Soon, days and nights, then weeks passed. The phases of the moon had gone from new to full to crescent, the last one being Jonathan's favorite.

The tide flowed in and out twice per day, filling the marsh then leaving it dry. But the boat never moved.

How strange, Jonathan thought, *especially for a boat. A boat in water is never still. Even when docked, a boat will float up and down in a symphony with the movement of the water surrounding it.*

His imagination took hold. Perhaps a family was living on the boat, and it was moored to an oyster bed. A mom, dad, little boy, and dog—just like Jonathan's family. Maybe they took a rowboat to shore each morning so the boy could go to school and the parents could buy groceries. Then at night, from the deck of their boat, they would listen to the tide roll in and roll slowly out, and to the oysters spitting under a full moon in the cool, briny breeze.

Jonathan asked his neighbors if they could see the boat from their houses too. Next door, Lily and Luca could see it. They thought it was a pirate ship!

According to them, the pirates were on vacation and parked their boat in the marsh. They came to play miniature golf, listen to music at the marina, sunbathe at the beach, and eat pizza. Once they rested up, they would stock their boat with supplies and take off on a new adventure.

That sounds like a nice vacation, Jonathan thought.

Down the street, Sophia could also see the boat. She told Jonathan the boat was haunted! One night, when the tide was high and smooth, Sophia and her mom had kayaked out to see the boat up close. Under the glow of the full moon, they could see the boat clearly; it was yellowed, dirty, and empty.

They heard spooky noises coming from inside the boat, and Sophia swore she had seen a ghost standing at the helm. Jonathan thought a haunted boat in the marsh was creepy. He hoped it wasn't true.

Grandma and Papa lived on the other side of the marsh. One afternoon, Jonathan came over with his yellow binoculars and he and Papa walked along the shoreline until they came upon a clearing in the marsh grass.

From this spot, they had a clear view of the boat—it was right in front of them! It was so close, they didn't even need binoculars to see it. And from here, they could see why the boat wasn't moving. It was tilted sideways, and its hull was stuck in the mud of a large oyster bed.

Papa believed that the boat had come untied from its dock during a hurricane. Maybe the boat had floated into the ocean, the wind and waves tossing it for miles and miles.

Eventually, the hurricane passed, but the boat was lost in the ocean, floating along until it took a turn at the lighthouse and ended up in its current resting place during low tide. Because no one had been there to drive the boat or take care of it, it ended up stuck in the mud—abandoned.

Jonathan was disappointed—no seafaring family, no pirates, no ghosts (thankfully).

Now what would happen?

Back at home, Jonathan thought about the day's discoveries. Whenever his toy trucks got stuck in the mud after a rainstorm, he was able to set them free by pulling them out of the mud and retracing their tracks in reverse to escape the mud's sticky embrace. Could he somehow pull the boat out of the mud and set it free too?

Jonathan studied all of the data he had collected about the boat over the last few weeks. With Rowan by his side, Jonathan brainstormed and sketched, slowly devising a plan he named Mission Muddy Paws. To set his plan into action, he would need the help of his friends Charlie and Sidney. They were skilled boaters and knew the waterways of the marsh. They even had their own boat named *Chuckles*. Jonathan called them and explained the situation. Charlie and Sidney were happy to help Jonathan with his mission, and they all agreed to meet at the marina the next morning at sunrise.

Jonathan woke up ready to take on the day. He brought Rowan and the plans he had sketched out. Charlie brought the naval maps of the marsh. Sidney had the tow ropes and equipment.

Their dads brought sunglasses and their moms brought the snacks. Then all of them boarded the *Chuckles* and took off. Mission Muddy Paws was underway!

The sun rose above the water, reflecting the dawn's cotton candy sky off the mirrored marsh. Pelicans dove gracefully for their breakfast. A blue heron watched from the shallow edge of the pluff mud as it disappeared with the growing tide.

They steered the boat into the main channel and cranked up the speed, laughing as the salty ocean spray tickled their cheeks and the wind rustled their hair.

Dolphins raced the *Chuckles* and splashed the kids, winking and grinning as they skipped along. And finally, after what seemed like forever, the abandoned boat lay ahead of them.

They pulled up next to the boat and tied the ropes to its cleats. This was the moment of truth. Would the *Chuckles* have enough power to pull the abandoned boat out of the muddy oyster bed just as the tide peaked?

Jonathan put the *Chuckles* into gear.

Heave! the *Chuckles* moaned in reply.

The boat teetered a tiny bit. Jonathan tried again.

HEAVE! said the *Chuckles*, this time sounding more powerful than the last.

The boat rocked again but settled back into the mud.

One more time, Jonathan hit full throttle and the *Chuckles* yelled, *HEAVE HO!* in reply.

This time, the abandoned boat came loose from the oyster bed and began to float as the tide grew higher and higher.

It was no longer stuck in the mud!

The *Chuckles* swiftly towed the boat all the way back to the marina. A large crowd had gathered to celebrate the rescue mission. Grandma and Papa were there, taking pictures. Regina and Michael cheered and held Nyo up for a better view of the action. Lily and Luca were there, wearing bandanas and eye patches just in case a pirate were along for the ride. Sophia smiled and waved, relieved that no ghost was found on the boat.

As they docked the boat, Jonathan thanked Charlie and Sidney and gave the *Chuckles* a tap on her hull. Mission Muddy Paws was complete, and it was a great success! Jonathan walked up the dock to the marina as an old-time boat captain named Captain Jack came up to shake his hand.

Captain Jack told Jonathan that in the ways of the water, the abandoned boat was now his very own boat to keep. Jonathan grinned ear to ear. His very own boat!

He knew a lot of work was ahead of him to get the boat up and running again. But of one thing he was certain: his boat would be named *Stuck in the Mud*.

South Carolina Seek!

1. Marshes, also called salt marshes, are some of the biggest ecosystems on Earth and are home to hundreds of living things. South Carolina has more marshes than any other state on the Atlantic coast.[1]

2. On average, there are seven hurricanes per year. They are named alphabetically from a list that the world meteorological organization established to make it easier for people to know which storm they are talking about.[2]

3. The tides of the ocean are controlled by the moon's gravitational pull on the Earth.[3]

4. There are eight moon phases throughout the month[4]:

New: We cannot see the moon.	**Full:** We can see the moon completely illuminated.
Waxing Crescent: In the Northern Hemisphere, we see this as a thin crescent of light on the right.	**Waning Gibbous:** This phase is between a full moon and a half moon. Waning means it is getting smaller.
First Quarter: We see a half moon.	**Third Quarter:** We see this as a half moon too, but it is the opposite half as is illuminated in the first quarter moon.
Waxing Gibbous: This phase is between a half moon and full moon. Waxing means it is getting bigger.	**Waning Crescent:** In the Northern Hemisphere, we see this as a thin crescent of light on the left.

5. Oysters are essential to the ecosystem of the marsh and feed by eating food particles. They are a filter for the water, and a healthy oyster can filter four gallons of water per hour.[5]

6. The pink birds in the book are the author's favorite! They are not flamingos but Roseate spoonbills. Of the six types of spoonbills in the world, this is the only one that lives in North America. Their long bill flattens out into the shape of a spoon for feeding, and they can be seen in the same marsh where the boat was located.[6]

7. Bottlenose dolphins are NOT fish, but actually the most common mammal found in estuaries and open water in South Carolina![7]

8. Can you spot the state tree of South Carolina that also gives it its nickname?[8]

9. There are two symbols that make up the state flag of South Carolina. Do you know what they are? Hint: Look at page 17 for clues![9]

10. Our illustrator is one of the people in the crowd waiting for Jonathan to tow in the boat. In real life, she is Jonathan's aunt and Godmother, and sister-in-law to the author of this book. Can you spot her?[10]

---

1 DNR.SC.Gov
2 NOAA.Gov
3 Moon.NASA.Gov
4 Spaceplace.NASA.Gov
5 DNR.SC.Gov
6 AllAboutBirds.com
7 DNR.SC.Gov
8 Answer: Sabal Palmetto Tree (pages 5, 11, 17, 18, 19, 24)
9 Answer: The Palmetto Tree and the Crescent Moon
10 Answer: On page 24, she's wearing a yellow shirt and red lipstick

About the Author and Illustrator

Brittany Sloan Fergus–Author

Stuck in the Mud is Brittany's first published book. Although she was born in Ohio, the marshy islands of South Carolina have called to her since childhood when she spent her family vacations at the shore. For a short time, Brittany and her family lived along the marsh where her son Jonathan's curiosity sparked the idea for *Stuck in the Mud*. The lowcountry of South Carolina is a magical place full of stories, and Brittany is happy that the story of *Stuck in the Mud* chose her to bring it to life. Nowadays, Brittany resides in Charlotte, North Carolina, with her husband Nathan and three sons Jonathan, Colin, and Ian.

The Story of *Stuck in the Mud*

The boy and the boat are real! A boat was really stuck in the marsh of Jonathan's backyard for several months. Jonathan became fascinated by the boat, and he would talk endlessly about it, question its purpose, and wonder what would happen to it. All of the curiosity gave me, his mom, an idea—to capture the excitement of this story for other children and adults with endless curiosity! And so the manuscript for *Stuck in the Mud* began. The neighborhood is a real neighborhood in South Carolina, and the neighbors and friends mentioned in the book are real too. Grandma and Papa still live on the island. With the help of neighbors and friends, many of whom were captured in the illustrations of this book, questions were answered and research was done to bring *Stuck in the Mud* to life. Special thanks to all of those who supported this effort, and a monumental thanks to my sister-in-law, Cait, for taking this project on with me and putting blood, sweat, and tears into the most beautiful illustrations I could ever imagine. Just a couple of moms turning a dream into reality. And a very special gift for a little boy named Jonathan from his mom and godmother.

Cait Chiou–Illustrator

Cait thinks kids are awesome. She works a fun parks and rec job with kids, volunteer teaches kids at her parish, is an enthusiastic aunt to a bunch of kids, and has four terrific kids of her own. This is Cait's first time illustrating a book about and for kids, and she loves it as well. Cait has an MFA in scenic design from Boston University and currently lives in the northwest suburbs of Chicago.

Printed in the USA
CPSIA information can be obtained
at www.ICGtesting.com
LVHW060344260124
769712LV00004B/122